J. M. Forrest

Columbus, an Historical and Romantic Drama

J. M. Forrest

Columbus, an Historical and Romantic Drama

ISBN/EAN: 9783337051976

Printed in Europe, USA, Canada, Australia, Japan

Cover: Foto ©Andreas Hilbeck / pixelio.de

More available books at **www.hansebooks.com**

AN HISTORICAL

—AND—

ROMANTIC DRAMA,

IN THREE ACTS,

—BY—

J. M. FORREST.

CHARLESTON, S. C.:
Edward Perry & Co., Printers and Stationers,
217 Meeting Street, Opposite Charleston Hotel.
1893.

COLUMBUS,

AN HISTORICAL AND ROMANTIC DRAMA,

IN THREE ACTS,

DRAMATIS PERSONÆ:

FERDINAND, King of Arragon.

ISABELLA, Queen of Castile.

PRINCE JUAN, Heir Apparent to both Crowns.

CHRISTOPHER COLUMBUS, Discoverer.

DIEGO,
FERNANDO, } Sons of Columbus.

BEATRIX ENRIQUES, Mother of Fernando.

DIEGO,
BARTHOLOMEW, } Brothers of Columbus.

FRIAR JUAN PEREZ, Prior of the Convent of La Rabida.

BISHOP FONSECA, Administrator of the Indies.

LUIS DE ST. ANGEL, Receiver of the Ecclesiastical Revenues in Arragon.

DON FRANCISCO DE BOBADILLA, Commissioner to San Domingo.

DON NICHOLAS DE OVANDO, Successor to Bobadilla.

DON ALONZO DE OJEDA, Daring Adventurer.

MARTIN PINZON, Navigator, Captain of the Pinta.

DON IGNACIO, Traitor to Columbus.

ESPINOSA, a Vile Wretch.

FRANCISCO ROLDAN, Conspirator.

DIEGO DE DEZA, Archbishop of Seville.

PROFESSOR, Couriers, Soldiers, Sailors, Prelates, Nobles, Indians, Showmen.

TUTOR, &c.

COLUMBUS.

ACT I.

SCENE 1. *Grounds in front of the Convent of La Rabida.*
Dim light in the windows. TIME. *A night in*
February (about 8 P. M.).

[*Columbus in troubled meditation paces to and fro.*
His young son is lying on the ground behind him asleep,
his head resting on an empty baskest.]

———————

COLUMBUS.
    Now the spangled frontage of the heavens
Roofs in the open temple of the night,
And silence tolls its psalm—it tolls proud hope
Of grand adventure to eternal rest.
      Later than the turn of the moon that's past,
I asked the King to grant a caravel
Or two, to try the venturous voyage.
He paused, then mumbled that the rapid needs
Of war conferred upon coin a double count.
Pray delay, he said, until that plenty-day
When the proud Alhambra's topmost tower
Strikes the unholy crescent to our flag,
Then your attendance I shall welcome once
Again. Crushed a seventh time in seven years,
I stood, run out of words. But as darkening clouds
That break not silence whilst they gather,
My silent soul gathered all its forces,
Then it rumbled 'gainst the sunshine of the King;
And in resenting thunders I humbled
For once, at least, the slippery majesty
Of Ferdinand. Seven wasted years
Outside the battlements of royalty
Have I lurked, and mixed with scullions, to learn
The ways and tempers of puffed officials,
Whose pompous intercessions were feathers
In a flaw, and deceptive obligations.

COLUMBUS.

From place to place, I followed the court,
And being much abroad, the vulgar called me
Show-struck, and the very children as I passed
Tapped their foreheads at the madman.
O Ferdinand of Arragon! Sage, Prince!
True soldier of the faith, my faith in thee
Hath wrought a ruin. When first I unveiled
The prospective dawn of empire beyond
The seas, your quick perception rose to ripe
Intent. Intent soon withered. In its dust
I have dragged a slimy snail track.

The golden Indies and their pearl-fringed coasts,
Spiced and scented lands, Solomon's mines
And all the glories of Marco Polo's words
I have offered to the reach of Spain. But Spain
Within Spain shall long remain. If she seeks
Columbus, she shall seek in vain.
Ho! Diego. Tired and sound asleep,
Filling your basket with nutritious dreams?
Diego, Ho! Diego, asleep?

DIEGO.

Yes, good father, out of bed I never slept before.

COLUMBUS.

Without a bed a sleep is better than
A bed without a sleep, as some hidalgos
Know.

DIEGO.

Without a bunk I dreamt a sailor's dream.

COLUMBUS.

A dream? How did it run?

DIEGO.

I dreamt you were in the Bay of Biscay tossed
And all the biscuits overboard were washed,
But you remembered that the waves forgot
A case of biscuits, hiding, piping hot.

COLUMBUS.

That's a lucky dream. The case of biscuits
Foreshadows plenty. But our case now is
Without the biscuits. With no venders here
For traffic, suppose we present our case
At the holy portal of this convent.

DIEGO.
>Our word the Fathers will not doubt.

COLUMBUS.
>Nor our looks.   Words are sometimes counterfeits,
>But looks are glimpses of the soul.   Come Diego,
>We must introduce ourselves.
>>>>(*Rings the convent bell.*)
>(*Enter Friar* JUAN PEREZ.)

FRIAR.
>Good strangers, peace and blessings to you both.
>What service is in the convent's gift that
>I can bestow?

COLUMBUS.
>Reverence! your words much needed cheer impart.
>Just now it would exceed a feast to give
>A drink of water and a little bread
>To my tired and foot-sore son.   For myself
>Want of appetite is not wanting.

FRIAR.
>We will contrive a better feast than that,
>But pray what urgency occasioned his fatigue?

COLUMBUS.
>Learning from report, some miles from Palos dwelt
>Substantial kindred of my lamented wife;
>We journeyed out on foot some days ago
>To test their nature for our name.   My aim
>In this distasteful quest is to obtain
>Aid, to gain a pass to France from Spain,
>Never to return again.

FRIAR.
>Your story draws a tide of thought.   Has France
>In your vocation run entirely short;
>Or has Spain a surplusage of worthy sons
>To cause your hasty unrest?

COLUMBUS.
>In Spain, through adverse winds of patronage,
>I'm denied not the rights of my vocation,
>But the rights of Spain therein.   Expansion
>Being now the policy of Arragon,
>A timely scheme I shaped to far exceed
>The utmost span of Ferdinand's desires.

COLUMBUS.

To him it offered an abounding profit;
For me abounding hazard it would yield.
But pauper counsel goes before the broom,
And oft the sweepings fertilize the fame
Of unentitled cheats.

FRIAR.

Attentive ear
I have bestowed and your cause I know not yet.
In honored confidence we speak, and hence
I would have your delicacy yield all
Clouded-up reserve. First, I would exact
The honor of your name; then all bearing
On your calling.

COLUMBUS.

As to my vocation,
'Tis at best but an offspring of the wind.
When with the wind, its rhumb line blithesome
    runs,
But like the changing looks of royalty
The wind, too, needs be humored, till with tact
And tacking the compass point is reached.
I'm a lover of the waves, the wind-kissed waves;
A seafarer, I am, wind and wave-worn;
An humble sailor, wishing for a name
To replace the unlucky one I have.

FRIAR.

What name is that?

COLUMBUS.

Columbus.

FRIAR.

Columbus! Memory reverberates
Most joyously at the ring of that name.
There lived in Lisbon, many years ago,
A stranger at whom science shook its head,
A most profound cosmographer he was,
And so deeply schooled in navigation,
He offered to carry the astrolabe
Over oceans yet unknown. His theories
Whirled storms through academical halls,
And the ruffled sages battled with their wits.

FRIAR.

Whether still lives this able theorist,
Or not, I have no warrant or account.
His name was Christopher Columbus.
Possibly, you have heard of him ?

COLUMBUS.

Yes, I have.

FRIAR.

He was married in Lisbon, I think.

COLUMBUS.

He was; so was I.

FRIAR.

He was a Genoese.

COLUMBUS.

And so am I.

FRIAR.

Now, I remember that once he appeared
Before the council of Salamanca.

COLUMBUS.

So did I; that is, so did he.

FRIAR.

(*Aside*) So did I; so did he. A surprise is at
hand.
Pray give me your Christian name ?

COLUMBUS.

Christopher.

FRIAR.

Then all points and particulars applied.
You must be a very counterfeit of,
If not, the celebrated navigator yourself.

COLUMBUS.

I am Christopher Columbus;
Known as a visionary and a fool,
In two countries, at least.

FRIAR.

I am silenced. That is enough. What's ours, is
yours.
The convent's hospitality accept,
And to-morrow some important men
Shall be assembled to entertain you.
Is this your only child ?

COLUMBUS.

The only one my lamented wife has left me.

FRIAR.

He will shine yet in the glitter of his proud name.

COLUMBUS.

Your assuring words make our hopes shine.

FRIAR.

The fingerpost of fate will shine to-morrow.
Now to 'scape the unwholesome dews of night
And being braced with consolation, to rest
We'll all retire. Follow me.

COLUMBUS.

(*Aside*) We are guests, not mendicants.

[*Exeunt.*]

(*Enter* BEATRIX ENRIQUEZ *with her young son* FERNANDO.)

BEATRIX.

Along the dismal road we toiled unseen,
Watching the wanderer. To this refuge
We have traced his footsteps. His perturbations
May find some calm in the restfulness of
This retreat. My poor presence here would but add
Fury to his sorrows; hence, I'll hide me
With my poor child in some brambled hollow
Of these grounds, and through the dewy leaves
Watch the morning's dawn. I am forgotten
By brave Columbus, but I am not dead.
His ponderous projects have entombed his love;
His golden Indies are coffined in his hopes,
And his life is but a leaden monument,
Crushing upon his mighty soul. His wrongs
Are mine, though mine in his concern are nought.
But anguish to-night is not incurable,
For the heavens are express in starry
(*She looks up at the heavens.*)
Combinations. True interpretation
Decrees a turn of fortune. Plainly read,
The forecast says, the angular distance
Twixt the moon and Cor Leonis shall be
(*Keeps looking at the sky, while she reads the stars.*)
Less painfully acute, and in good time
Shall be right-angled. Then, here is the moon,
There is Cor Leonis. Heavenly portents!

BEATRIX.

(*Points to herself, then to the convent, then looks up at the sky.*)

A new star, that is a new world. A world
By infallible sign shall be discovered !
Then trumpets shall sound, Columbus shall
    triumph,
His glory shall thunder the land and sea.
The rocks shall be chiseled and lifted
To give him the Earth's veneration.
My exultations shall fling my last sigh
Into the multitudinous roar
Of the joyous Earth. But girlhood is past
And unrelished womanhood has settled on me.
The romp, and all the tiny freaks that make
The mountains of a girl's joys are past.
Undrowsed, I drank of the deep expoundings
Of Columbus, and struggled with tangents,
Angles and degrees, till my little brain
Lost all its spring and bound. But my tutor
Fondled to my earnestness, and I was earnest
In love for him. But night grows apace,
And the moon must now to her quarters hie.
Come, Fernando, let us now discover
Where discovery least invites. I see it.
Yonder thicket is the place. We'll away.

                   [*Exeunt.*]

(BEATRIX *has faith in astrology ; she reads the stars.*)

--- -- -- --

SCENE 2.   *A Public Road.*

(*Enter Two Couriers.*)

1ST COURIER.

Didn't the King look war and wonder at us
As he shot his words into our errand ?

2ND C.

He looked to me all reddened to the scalp.
The tears of toil rolled down from every pore,
As if he had been ditching.

1st C.
> Ditching moors.
> The moors he'll ditch till the ghost of Islam
> Has jumped the straits.

2nd C.
> Gibralter and the straits
> We shall jump if we fail to find Columbus.

1st C.
> Find, but catch him not, unless in the act
> Of leaving Spain, are the King's strict commands.

2nd C.
> Suppose that now outside the bounds of Spain
> He dwells; would that mean banishment or death
> For us?

1st C.
> Worse, I fear. Dungeons dark, irons,
> Musty rations, vanishing anatomy,
> And our sepulchral bones rattling for death
> Would be our lot.

2nd C.
> Then 'tis time to climb the highest tree, or drop
> Down the tallest chimney.

1st C.
> Be collected, your fortitude renew,
> Here comes a stranger, we'll sound him for a clue.

(Enter old Professor, hurrying past to meet his class.)

> Worthy gentleman, with salutations
> Most respectful, we humbly approach you
> To win from your wisdom some advice.

PROFESSOR.
> The wrong man you have not met.
> Right questions, wrong answers ne'er beget,
> Nor evasions breed. Hasten and proceed.

1st C.
> Most distinguished sir, from your sage remarks,
> We judge that Doctor Spitlingo you must be,
> Or, perhaps you are not.

PROFESSOR

 I am expositor of multifarious arts
And concatenated incognoscibilities.
Five and twenty sciences I expound,
And give gloss and finish to a multitude
Of costly accomplishments, such as law,
Medicine, and the flute. A class of students
Now await my clear elucidations
Of those complex transcendantal questions
Which would liquify the shell in which your brains
Now rattle.

2ND C.

 (*Aside*). The class is waiting.

1ST C.

 (*Aside, silence!*) My friend in prayer, is given to
  ejaculating.
Most learned Doctor, in a limited sense,
We comprehend the vastness of your mind.
Your apprehension we shall not blind
With winding fables. Our business then:
Commissioned, we have been by our master,
Who is the most exalted in the land,
To search these kingdoms for a wandering,
But gifted man, whose name is Columbus.

PROFESSOR.

 It cannot be Christopher Columbus?

1ST C.

 The same.

PROFESSOR.

 I can offer the best authority
For stating, that he is at the convent
Down the road. Perhaps, in holy orders,
He intends to end his days.

2ND C.

 That ends our orders and musty rations.

1ST C.

 Tush man! tighten up your wits.
Excuse the pious ejaculations of my friend;
He bubbles thus all day.

PROFESSOR.

> I am in haste.   The class is waiting.
> But I'll sum up Columbus before I go.
> Impossible theories have crazed him.
> Why should he suppose that the Earth is round?
> Why may not the Earth exhibit the divers
> Bulges of the human skull, plus the plump
> Carbuncles of the physiognomy.
> We live upon the physiognomy.
> The eyes are volcanoes; the hypotheneuse
> Of the nose is an alpine ridge; the whiskers
> Primeval forests; and the mouth agape
> Is the Mediterranean sea.   And out 'pon
> The Earth's skull no living thing can live.

2ND C.

> The class is waiting.

1ST C.   (*Aside—shameful*).

> > Most learned Doctor,
> We are profoundly struck.

PROFESSOR.

> > I can strike you dumb.
> Suppose the Earth's huge skull on my shoulders.
> Observe how the occiput is braced
> By a conchoidal-cissoid curving under
> The great trapezium which crushes up
> The polar axis of the cranium.   Then sweeping
> Down the great hyperborean region,
> A bold hyperbolical curve lashes
> The occidental knob, from the summit
> Of which, an accurate horizontal
> Parallax might be taken.   Dipping thence
> Into a double hypotrochoid which links
> A flying quadratrix with the drooping
> Catenary of the bristled chin completes
> Three-fifths of *quod erat demonstrandum.*

(*Takes off his hat and applies his hand to his head while descriting*).

> What does Columbus know about that?
> Could he approximate a surd?

1ST C.

> It is absurd.

2ND C.
                        It really is, 'pon my word,
    Diabolical.
1ST C.
                        My friend at prayer again,
    Ejaculating.
PROFESSOR.
                        The class is waiting.
    But on the black-board with chalk, I could sweep
    You and Columbus 'round the Earth, and sketch
        you
    As hanging antipodes, with your skulls
    Glancing up at your vamps, like unto
    Falling angels with all the blood and marrow
    In your heads, cut loose upon your descending
    Expedition to parts unknown. Just as
    Columbus wants to do.
1ST C. (*Aside*).
    Close his volcanoes with a sweep of your hand!
    Make an antipode of him! Land him
    On his skull!
PROFESSOR.
    The wind hath changed a quarter point,
    Bringing with it a moistened cloud which plays
    Painfully upon an osseous formation
    On my littlest toe. Therefore, punctual
    Time, to keep with my expectant class,
    I will depart with quick but limping step.
    I will gratify your appreciative ears
    Soon again with profounder views. Adieu.
                                        [*Exit.*]
1ST C.
    Health and happiness! Adieu.
2ND C.
    His due would be to bruise his osseous formation.
    That old spluttermug is crazy. The buffer
    Knows nothing of where Columbus is. Let us
    Go in search at once.
1ST C.
    You think so? You may be right.
    Let us learn for ourselves.

2ND C.
    We should have done so sooner, instead
    Of gaping at that scuttled skull maniac. Then
      away!

                [*Exeunt.*]

SCENE.- *Front of Alhambra Palace During the Surrender
of Granada.* (*Shots heard inside. Drums, bugles*).
Dead and dying on the ground. (*Bustle, Ambulances,
&c.*). *Enter the King, surrounded by officers. A
Courier in attendance.*

KING (*to Courier*).
    Place a saddle upon the wind, or find
    A swifter horse than that which bore my last
    Dispatch. Carry this important message
    To the Queen, and acquaint her majesty
    In your own words of all that you have seen
    Of the storming and surrender. Tell her
    We witnessed the lowering of the crescent,
    Heard the last shot fired, have the Alhambra
    And all the forts in hand, and Boabdil
    In safety ; and that in the panic
    The city's needs have been generously met.
    Speed your way and ere the blink of twilight
    Find me at the Alhambra with return news.

                [*Exit Courier*].
      (*To officers and soldiers*).

Comrades in arms! Once again a Spaniard,
A Spaniard is, for Spain belongs to Spain.
This day the historian lays down his pen.
The story of eight hundred years is ended.
During eight centuries the swarming vampires
Have sucked the veins and arteries of Spain,
And have left our skeleton in the school-books,
Nothing better than a tradition. Now
The multitudinous resurrection
Of our race, shall as much surprise the Earth
As it has confounded our enemy.

KING.

    No more symbols, signs, or shows of Islam
Shall defile our land. Yet from our captives,
Mercy measured with a leaning balance,
Shall not be withheld. War resounds no more.
Its smoke, turned to golden clouds, canopies
A jubilee of peace. Nothing remains
For us who hold direction of affairs
But to administer with collective wisdom
Our long lost, well won province. Let the troops
Relieved from action defile before us,
That we may exchange greetings and observe
Their exulting pride [*aside*]. Our plenty-day has
    come.
Now for Columbus!

                (*Review, music, cheers, &c.*).

SCENE.—*A public street. Enter Punchinello and Pipes
(two strolling showmen), from opposite sides.*

PUNCH.

    War and thunder, brother showman; that's not
    you?

PIPES.

    Slight mistake, if it's not.

PUNCH.

    Where have you been starring it, past five years?

PIPES.

    Under ground, part of the time.
    Where have you been?

PUNCH.

    Just escaped. Wrenched a lock, forced a bolt,
Filed a chain, bored a six foot hole.
Couldn't digest hard tack.
Who rammed you underground?

PIPES.

    No one. It was voluntary compulsion.
Within the walls of Granada I stayed
While the raging siege progressed. The maddened
Moors resolved to spike all Spaniards in the town.

PIPES.

Taking the hint, I took a bucket too,
And jumped the bucket with myself
Down into a well, full forty feet in depth,
And bumped on rats and reptiles whose thirsty
shrieks
Told that the well was dry. After twenty-seven
days,
Welcome shouts of triumphant Spaniards rang,
I climbed to daylight and here I am again.

PUNCH.

The law was out of order, you will judge
In my case. I started two fandango fellows
Before a sick man's house, to wring some coins
From his agony. He showered the money out
To get us off. I then redoubled ·
The racket of the pipes to worry him,
But instead of sending out more money,
He sent for the officers of the law,
Who grasped and chucked me, while my partners
Vanished with the cash.

PIPES.

I stifle to think that our profession
Should have come under the bludgeon of the law.

PUNCH.

Did it ever strike you that our profession
Is rattling down the hill?

PIPES.

Yes; it struck me insensible at the bottom
Of the well.

PUNCH.

I grieve to observe that third-class impostors
Are imitating our entertainment.

PIPES.

Bad enough; but blame the war more than all.
The lower orders of the Moors always
Patronized our entertainments.
To catch the upper classes, a slow broken bone
Lamentation was just the thing. The Moors
Are now down, and we may fling the pipes
And Punchinello on top of them.

PUNCH.
> Hold! here comes an angel with two children.

(Enter Beatrix and two children passing along).

> Pardon, gracious madam, our overflowing
> Desire to gratify the little hearts of children.
> Our show being chaste, they can look, laugh, and
> listen,
> And investigate free of all expense.

BEATRIX.
> Accept the expense.   You can owe them
> The amusement.   *(Gives them money).*

*(While Punch is speaking, Pipes stands aloof, gazing in
wonder at Beatrix).*

> We are pressed for time.

PIPES *(aside).*
> Madam, pardon one word more.   Startled
> By your resemblance to a most distinguished
> Lady whom my sister nursed, impelled, I feel
> To speak.   Many generations of her race
> My family have served, in humble grade.

BEATRIX.
> Whereto, belonged those people of whom you
> speak ?

PIPES.
> Cordova.

BEATRIX.
> Their name.

PIPES.
> Enriquez.
> The youngest daughter, Beatrix, was by
> My sister nursed.   My father her father's
> Tasty gardener was ; and as trusty coachman
> My grandfather drove a noted span for
> Her grandfather.

BEATRIX.
> What is your name ?

PIPES.
> Espinosa.

BEATRIX.

> That the strict breeding of a sobered home,
> Should have cast off a fantastic rover
> Like you, seems strange.

PIPES.

> A restless boyhood drifted me to sea.
> By savage pirates I was then enslaved.
> I tricked their vigilance, and from bondage
> Tore to the open sea again. A ship-wreck
> Changed the current of my thoughts, and I roved
> For years upon the land, blowing the horn
> At times, for the royal mail. A showman
> I then bought out. This is my career.

BEATRIX.

> You are a man of honor without reward.
> Perhaps your lucky hour has come. Would money
> Tempt you to the sea again?

PIPES.

> Any day for good pay I am ready.

BEATRIX.

> Then come aside. You can cage a secret?
> I am Beatrix Enriquez.
> These are children of Columbus.
> I am conveying them to court unknown
> To him. You have heard of Columbus?

PIPES.

> Many and many a time.

BEATRIX.

> Talk is rife again about his expedition.
> Should his canvas spread, I shall have on board
> Observant eyes to play the faithful watch.
> The place is yours. Like your messmates you
>   must
> Also play the sailor. But secretly
> You shall make in briefest diction a record
> Daily of every incident of moment
> To Columbus. Note his orders, tone of voice,
> The cloud and sunshine on his looks;
> His health, appetite, and snatching slumbers.
> And above all his joys, if any, he reveals.
> His joys are the dress garments of my poor love.

BEATRIX.

> Alas! my love is charted as a reef,
> Or quicksand by him, but second soundings
> Will prove it the sunken wreck of affection.
> I am comforted now at meeting one
> Of the time-tried followers of my kindred
> In whom I can confide. To-morrow, dawn,
> You will meet me again, where this card instructs.
>   (*Gives him a card*).
> If worthy, your comrade might share my friend-
> ship, too.

PIPES.

> I am all action without prattle.
> Prattlers and tattlers were scarce in my family.

BEATRIX.

> Time is pressing. Come children, we must away.
> Adieu.   [*Exit*].

(*While* PIPES *is speaking with* BEATRIX, PUNCH *is enlight-
ening the children on the mysteries of the show*).

PUNCH.

> Who was that meek inspiration?

PIPES.

> Can you cage a secret?

PUNCH.

> Yes; and I can stitch it in the lining
> Of my coat.

PIPES.

> Whisper. She's a discovery.

PUNCH.

> Has she discovered on us? Any danger?

PIPES.

> Danger and discovery are sometimes
> Fields of fortune.

PUNCH.

>   Yes, I have found them so,
> When discovery of danger, disclosed
> The danger of discovery.

PIPES.
> Danger or. death,
> I am going to discover something.
> I shall auction off the pipes and jingling bobs.
> I am into a prime game of go-between
> With money on both sides. Between my claws
> The lovers shall feel a squeeze.

PUNCH.
> Why not give your chum a chance? I'll give you
>> points.

PIPES.
> We'll talk it over. Bring your traps along.
> Your companionship may yield some
> Cunning hints.
>> [*Exeunt*].

SCENE—*Interior of La Ribida.* COLUMBUS, PRIOR JUAN
PEREZ, MARTIN PINZON, DOCTOR FERNANDEZ, &c.

FRIAR.
> Her majesty I found at Santa Fe,
> In that gracious mood which is hers alone.
> Being a former penitent of mine,
> Her royal presence reproduced old joys.
> Welcome I expected, but more I received,
> And to your advantage very much indeed.
> Isabella rose to bounding plaudits
> As her voice mounted to your bold conceptions.
> She expressly charged, without stop or stay,
> That you at court present yourself in person,
> To instruct her in your plans, requirements,
> And the possibilities of results.
> In your approval lies your own success.

COLUMBUS.
> I must decline, finally, for ever.
> A month or two ago had Ferdinand
> Thrown me his pockethandkerchief in jest,
> I would have carried it to the mast-head
> As a flag, and proudly dared the ocean
> With a ten ton caravel. Worlds were cheap
> When a worthless rag could have fired adventure.
> Since then new worlds have sobered in their rates.

COLUMBUS.

Values have advanced far beyond the reach
Of Arragon. That which I propose to find
I shall carry to a foreign mart for sale.
Glory, debased by profit, may not yield
Sweet rhymes to poets. But rhymes and glory
Have no stalls in market. Therefore, I'll strike
A sharp bargain with those who will but trade.

FRIAR.

Know you, now Columbus,
That you have not to treat with Arragon.
Your fortune lies in Castile. Commission,
Ships, seamen, and supplies, a protecting flag,
And a cheering smile for a fair wind,
Are all yours from good Queen Isabella's heart.
The monarchs are united by sacred
And domestic ties, but Isabella
Rules Castile. You will meet a sailor, a Plato,
A Cæsar, and an angel, in the Queen.

COLUMBUS.

Kind Father, just when night was blackest,
And the dismal journey of life was crossed
By puzzling and unfamiliar paths, you,
By inscrutible destiny, arose
At the point whereat I paused, and led me
Into the pleasant sunshine of hope.
I am not short of gratitude, but of terms
In which to word it. Your words have saved me
From my blind intentions. Your careful soundings
At Santa Fe have given me a chart,
But above all, you have paid the ransom
Of my imprisoned pride, by acting for me.
And now my will is yours, with this single
Reservation, that I myself dictate
The terms, if I am commissioned.

FRIAR.

The means to the end can be proportioned
By you alone.

PINZON.

Reverend Father, my interposition
You will forgive. In your absence, talking
With our honored friend, Columbus, upon

PINZON.

    This self-same question of ways and means,
    I diffidently let slip the offer
    Of a seventy-ton first-class caravel,
    To assist in any expedition
    With Columbus in command. A sea-boat,
    Worthy of the waves, she's named the Pinta,
    And I, her captain, will gladly guide her
    Wherever Columbus leads.

COLUMBUS.

    Captain Pinzon, our friendship is sealed.
    Should Isabella prove half as willing
    As the Captain of the Pinta, the port
    Of Palos, soon will ring with departing cheers.

FRIAR.

    Then it is agreed that we have agreed
    On immediate action.

COLUMBUS.

    Action, if no reaction chills the royal will.

PINZON.

    Reaction and inaction were buried
    In the fall of Grenada. At present,
    Action is the word that applies in Spain.

FRIAR.

    Then let us act forthwith, each to his work.
    But friends, all, let us first repair
    To our humble oratory for a parting prayer.
                           [Exeunt].

SCENE.—*Private Chamber in the Palace.* KING FERDI-
        NAND *and* LUIS ST. ANGEL.

FERDINAND.

    With all our glory I am dismayed by dark
    Forebodings.

ST. ANGEL.

    The sum of triumph, comes not to the grasp at
        at once. Sometimes
    Like fern leaves, the results of war fructify
    On the back ; the seeds unseen in propagation
    Thrive, and in time the land becomes enriched.

FERDINAND.

    How, if sudden blight should blast all the seeds?
    Noxious omens now are being wafted round.

ST. ANGEL.

    Being exalted, your majesty's ken extends beyond
        Ours
    In many things. To common Spanish hearts
    The prospect could not present more comfort.

FERDINAND.

    Comfort if nothing lay beyond. See that
    Pompous stretching of the limbs at Lisbon.
    'Tis meant for might and mettle, but is envy
    In disguise. From us no active notice
    Is demanded, but Spain must keep her eye
    Upon our little neighbor.

ST. ANGEL.

    Confronting possibilities, the safest
    Statecraft is: A poodle pup fattened
    Into impudence is not a mastiff;
    His barking at our heels is more fun than fright.

FERDINAND.

    Suppose that poodle should shed all his fleece
        except
    The mane, and give a lion's roar. How then?

ST. ANGEL.

    Let all the lions loose that your majesty
    Loosened on the Moors.

FERDINAND.

    Observation at present, and provision
    'Gainst insecurity for the future
    Is our best policy. It is plain to all
    That rapid aggrandizement from discoveries
    Has given vigor to the whole face
    Of Portugal. Where are we upon the seas?
    Pay and bounty must drive our fleets abroad
    Or else we must recede and brook dictation.

ST. ANGEL.

    Outside empire, if any still remains,
    Be it rock or region, shall own your flag
    By the simple sanction of your word.

FERDINAND.

Outside our word 'twould take some magic means
To give us that accrument.

ST. ANGEL.

We have one daring spirit in our midst,
With thoughts unborrowed, and too big to lend;
Who can locate a land of gold, his eyes
Have never seen. I vouch he can, from proof
His words have given.

FERDINAND.

You mean Columbus?

ST. ANGEL.

I do.

FERDINAND.

I know the man as an apparition
In my thoughts. He has dogged us with his vast
And tedious theories; and approached us
Only when the risks of war strained our thoughts.
With something sharper than a sword, I cut
His theories short. If his soul is hurt,
The healing time is come. We'll make amends.

ST. ANGEL.

To rekindle his esteem, reparation's
Easiest course would be a royal order
To proceed to sea at once.

FERDINAND.

That order I cannot give. No party
Can I be to an enterprise which hangs
As much on chance as on the sailor's skill.
Failure would wreck our prestige.

ST. ANGEL.

Hold your sanction till it has succeeded.
The means to float it is what is needed.

FERDINAND.

It will acquit us best, perhaps, to leave
All arrangements to the Queen. Twice she spoke
Of summoning Columbus to the court
To learn from his lips the positive
And the very doubtful certainties of his scheme.
I would have your counsel assist her
Should Columbus present himself at court;
Her sanction should not run too lavish.

ST. ANGEL.

    Between business and benevolence
Her majesty can draw the line. To profit
By her wisdom, I shall attend upon her,
And will suggest, if anything is forgotten.

FERDINAND.

    We are competitors for the world's trade,
And it is true new territory we covet,
But that from the barbarian only.
Find him where we may, by Christendom un-
    claimed,
In palms, or golden filigree attired,
We shall trim his traditions and clothe him
In the fashions of a new existence.

ST. ANGEL.

    Sound in wisdom every word. But to end
Small measurings I say, Columbus westward
Let him sail. Discovery's the thing.

FERDINAND.

    Then let Columbus have the chance he craves.
His nature's paradox being rashly right,
Fits him for the work. His words sound sagely,
But as ripples are no gauge of depth, drop
A well-greased lead into his theories,
Humor his ambition with assurance
Of honors on his triumphant return.
Above all, place his loyalty beyond
The touch of our neighbor's envy. At once
To the Queen repair. Columbus may be
In audience at this moment.

ST. ANGEL.

    Your royal words in rekindling echo
Shall be rendered to her majesty.
The tide is with us. Yea, the awaiting flood
Is more momentous than that which carried
Cæsar and his fortunes. Every ebb of tide
Now counts against us. To the Queen forthwith !
                        [Exit].

FERDINAND.
>Two uncommon citizens! a prophet
>And a discoverer. Whether the waves
>Our words bemoan or loudly verify,
>We shall the meanwhile spend the interest
>Of that fictitious capital called hope.
>But the rank unwholesome Moorish question
>Has left unfinished work, which strains the
>>strength
>Of all our thoughts. A train of sturdy
>Measures must be enforced to end the question
>Forever and forever. [*Exit*].

COLUMBUS *before* ISABELLA *at Santa Fe. Present—*
Nobles, Prelates, Sage Professors, and
distinguished Ladies.

ISABELLA.
>Christopher Columbus, our inaction
>During the interlapse, since your first appeal,
>Was caused by the turmoil and financial
>Drain of protracted war. To make amends
>Now, we have summoned you to our presence.
>Your bold proposals in all their bearings,
>Given from your own lips, will best satisfy
>Our judgment. You shall supremely govern
>Our whole attention, by now proceeding
>With any method of instruction you may adopt.
>>(*Enter* LUIS ST. ANGEL).

COLUMBUS.
>Your most gracious majesty, descrying
>The golden-Indies would be an ecstacy,
>But the pride of discovery would not
>Half compare with the exalted pleasure
>Imparted by your royal and befriending
>Words. To the whole world it is no secret
>That your majesty has a generous heart;
>Therefore, I have made no discovery.
>But to gratify that heart, discovery
>I shall bestow, if sanction is vouchsafed.
>In bringing my theories before you,
>I shall strike all philosophy from them,

COLUMBUS.
Save the points that failed at Salamanca.
First point: are antipodes impossible
If the earth is round. Ptolemy says no.
He belts the Earth with four and twenty hours,
And fifteen of these he precisely gives
To the extended arc that joins Thinæ
In Asia, to the Canaries' ancient group.
One hour more to the Azores, makes sixteen,
And makes all of the world that now is known.
I propose to find the eight hours missing,
Which in degrees, six score measure. 'Tis plain
If our race can swarm with an all-angled
Footing upon a curve, twelve score degrees,
They can hold the remaining arc. But still
We are asked is the world round. Shadows an-
swer that.
But a sailor's proof is deemed the simplest.
Before he sights the ship itself, he sees
The lofty sails. Next blurted question is:
Are the glittering Indies fiction
To make the toddlings gape. The answer must
come
From the very lips of the illustrious dead.
Marco Palo, who had seen the roofs of gold,
The golden stairway, the hundred thousand
Elephants, all caparisoned in gold,
And the dazzing profusion of precious stones,
Was asked upon his dying bed to retract
His statements. He said no. After him
The noble Mandeville swept the Indies,
And others followed, and their narratives
Endorse each other. Marco Palo went
By an eastern route. I propose to go
By a western route to plant the banners
Of your majesties in the golden Indies.
ISABELLA.
Columbus, enough; decision is reached.
We are convinced. You may forthwith proceed
With active preparations. I hereby
Assume the whole responsibility
And cost of the expedition on the part

ISABELLA.

> Of my own crown exclusively. The funds
> By personal sacrifice shall be found.
> My jewels shall be pawned and the proceeds
> To your credit written.

ST. ANGEL.

> I beg to assure your generous majesty
> That for this sacrifice there is no need.
> That money can be advanced from the funds
> Of Arragon, I have authority to state.

ISABELLA.

> Either way will equally please.

COLUMBUS.

> With most profound respect and highest
> Sense of gratitude, I thank your majesty
> For your most enlightened action.
> It now becomes my duty to submit
> The terms on which I accept your commission.
> To compel strict obedience in the fleet,
> I demand the title of admiral
> Of the Spanish seas. To gain submission
> From strange peoples, I demand the title
> And dignities of viceroy of the lands
> I shall discover; and in addition,
> I demand one-tenth of all the products
> And trade of said lands in perpetuity.

ST. ANGEL.

> Columbus, her majesty's approval
> Reflects the King's. For both, I say your demands
> Are outside compliance. Should your venture
> Come to nothing, titles would be mere sounds
> Without rank. Titles should succeed success.

COLUMBUS.

> Every means essential to my enterprise
> I have well considered, and the result
> Is given in the conditions named.
> Before embarking from the shores of Spain
> I shall humbly claim a royal patent
> Embodying all my rights and titles.
> The imperishable parchment engrossed
> In Roman letters, and not a letter less,
> Shall be my credentials to the grand Kahn
> Of all the Indies.

ISABELLA.

    I do think Columbus should be clothed
    With superior power to compel respect
    From his warrior seamen. Concessions
    Most generous we are willing to make.

ST. ANGEL.

    These shrewd claims so suddenly announced
    Call for consideration.

COLUMBUS.

    I shall all abandon, or insist.
    No compromise.

ST. ANGEL.

    Then I propose immediate conference
    With the King. That will satisfy us all.

COLUMBUS.

    Satisfied I am, if I am satisfied.

ISABELLA.

    Now Columbus, the time is come to say
    Goodbye. Take this little cross for my sake
    To the dismal seas, and in tempest and
    Solicitude, it will remind you that
    The seas are swept by the merciful eye
    Of Him who died for you. Health! Safety!
    And a triumphant return! Adieu!

COLUMBUS.

    With that cross, your majesty, other crosses
    Shall be overcome.

ST. ANGEL.

    Now to the King for conference.

                                 (All withdraw).

ACT II.

Barcelona.—Scene.—*A Street. In centre a public font surmounted by statue, behind which Beatrix secretly listens. Time—Midnight. Enter* Don Ignacio (*in disguise*) *and Espinosa.*

IGNACIO.

Out with it now, this deserted byway sleeps.
None can hear us ; minutes count.

ESPINOSA.

Come, funnel up your ears, and I'll fill you up
With sea-water, notes, and memoranda
Splashed from the admiral's own log. No lie.
That log is mine ; a mine of gold it's worth.
This is the fourtune treacherous Pinzon lost.
He deserted Columbus, and steered home
To be the first to trumpet to the court
The great discoveries, and claim the prize.
This book opens the road to the new world
Without the company of Columbus.
I, therefore, am the richest man in Spain.

IGNACIO.

How fell this precious record to your luck ?

ESPINOSA.

Too full of wonder am I now to tell.

IGNACIO.

To kill impatience burst the wonder quick.

ESPINOSA.

There may be profit in patience. Attend :
Now I know nothing about azimuth,
Longitude, and angular distance.
But this book is crammed with these ocean mile-
    stones,
Which mark the unerring path for ships to sail.
You or I can reach the new world now.

IGNACIO.

Did Columbus rejoice at finding land ?

ESPINOSA.

    Yes; and our hardships were ejected from our heads
    By the novelty of the scene.

IGNACIO.

    Did he name the place first sighted?

ESPINOSA.

    Yes; being fond of prayers and holy names,
    He called it the Island of San Salvador.

IGNACIO.

    On your return to Spain did Palos fling
    Her hugging arms round you?

ESPINOSA.

    Yes; her arms took our legs from under us.
    Tossed we were as first-born babes into the air.
    The whole journey from Palos to Barcelona
    Was one foaming wine-drinking, trumpeting
    Triumph.

IGNACIO.

                You will show your shining buttons
    In to-morrow's triumphal procession?

ESPINOSA.

    Yes; all who have returned from the Indies
    Will escort Columbus and the Indians
    Through the streets.

IGNACIO.

                You will return to the Indies?

ESPINOSA.

    Never as a sailor; perhaps, as a speculator.

IGNACIO.

    Well, suppose that I speculate in that book,
    And that you speculate with the gold exchange?

ESPINOSA.

    Where is your cloud-capt mountain of gold
    With which to buy it? Pooh! if I go to any
    Of the hangers-on round the court, such as
    Bobadilla, Ovando, or De Ojeida,
    They will sack the royal mint and give me
    Barrows of bullion for one single peep
    At this guide to the land of gold.

IGNACIO.

O, come to business. How to your luck
Did this log book chance to fall?

ESPINOSA.

That's a history. A scapegrace life
I lived for many years; at last I chanced
To meet a mystery—a love struck lady.
She idolized no less a person than
Columbus. In vain she schemed at playing
The stowaway in the Santa Maria.
But detection fearing, with bribes she tempted me
To ship, and play the watch. With her name in-
    scribed,
That vapory maiden handed me this book.
In it I was to make a daily note
Of every action, mood and emotion
Of Columbus, to soothe her pining soul.
I jumped on board and chuckeled. Then threw
    the book
Under the keen eye of the Admiral.
As if the dead had risen he whitened
At reading Beatrix Enriquez
On the first page. I claimed the book, and more
I claimed the lady as the benefactress
Of my humble family. His heart burst bounds.
I was made admiral's valet with charge
Of all private papers and the log.

IGNACIO.

Then you stole the log?

ESPINOSA.

No; from it I made a daily copy
Of every recorded observation, for outward
And return voyage. This is the copy
And true log.

IGNACIO.

You have deceived Columbus and the lady.

ESPINOSA.

Yes; I have. But think you, that I who had
    prowled
In the raw winds of poverty and lain
In the lairs of hounded thugs, and smut clouts,
Could have suddenly recast my nature

ESPINOSA.

    To compile a cupid's love-book, for this
    Fitful damsel, to construe her dreams by?
    No; I risked my life for fortune; let him
    Who will, give his life for glory.

IGNACIO.

    Some royalty of soul sparkles in your words.
    When honesty becomes enriched by toil,
    Its independence is storm-proof.

ESPINOSA.

    Sir, you do me justice. My true motives
    Being not misunderstood, breeds an inward
    Satisfaction.

IGNACIO.

    Our sympathies entwining for mutual good
    Prove us as well matched as nature's twins.

ESPINOSA.

    May this healthy friendship never need a drug.

IGNACIO.

    Gilded pills are the drugs for enmity.
    Each the other we, in barter may outbid,
    But he who bids for one, must buy us both.

ESPINOSA.

    Your lusty frankness is a cue to business.
    To a midnight tavern let us quickly trip
    And with a flask of wine place this treasure (the
        book)
    In the scales.

IGNACIO.

    Agreed.

ESPINOSA.

    You know Barcelona? Is there an open house?

IGNACIO.

    Yes; two turns of the street will bring the sign
    Of the Caravel in sight, where good wines,
    A rosy widow, and welcome can be found.

ESPINOSA.

    Then let us thither, away.   [*Exeunt*].

    (*Enter* BEATRIX *from behind the Font*).

BEATRIX.

Angels of heaven disarm my vengeance
Whilst I pursue these demons. The ghoul-eyed
Slimy spiders now spread their midnight mesh
To catch their incautious prey. To entangle
The brave Columbus is their aim. Round me
Already the poisoned coils are wreathed,
But the sleepless sentinels who keep watch
Over unwary souls, will blast the plot,
And cast the shame of daylight upon the rogues.
The iron knaves, with swine-fat phrases rub
Each other. I'll track them to hear the last
Syllable of their reeking spume, though death
Doth follow.   [*Exit*].

SCENE.—*A vast and magnificent Saloon in the Royal
Palace of Barcelona. Thrones under a rich canopy
of brocade of gold. King, Queen, and* PRINCE JUAN
*seated. A throng of nobles, cardinals, and Court
dignitaries. Enter* COLUMBUS *accompanied by Indians. All kneel down, and the Te Deum Lauda-
mus is sung.*

KING FERDINAND.

Admiral Columbus, in greeting you
Be it ordained, you being our most honored
     subject,
That your presence suspends all ceremony.
Take your seat.

COLUMBUS.

                    Your gracious majesty
Has not only given me rank, but also
Undergrades to rule. The respect I exact
From them, I in turn render unto you.
Therefore, in conformity with discipline,
I stand before your majesties.

FERDINAND.

Which way you will before us, before the world
You sit enthroned, and crowned. In history
No event can confront your achievement.

FERDINAND.

Legion against legion gave Cæsar conquests;
A debauch gave Babylon to Cyrus;
The prattle of geese shook Brennus at Rome,
But the prattle of the grim engulfing
Ocean, dismayed you not. No chance or trick
Of fortune threw a tow-line to your hopes.
Your little timbers bounded 'gainst the legions
Of howling billows, until destiny
Compelled a final triumph. This day Spain
Garlands her affections round a hero's brow.
She has given you a Roman triumph.
No Zenobia dragged in golden chains
Sighed behind your triumphal car. No spoils
From temples and strongholds were marshaled into
Your glittering pageant. You are not
A Hannibal, for you have not returned
To Carthage with the pecks of jeweled rings.
Only the simple products of the soil
And treasures of the mines you have brought.
These are more to Spain than the gloried trophies
Of Rome or Macedon. This great event
Makes every voice a trumpet; and forever
Shall its multitudinous echo be heard.
Columbus, accept the nation's gratitude,
And spare us not in all requirements
For your future deeds.

COLUMBUS.

On deck in clamoring winds, better can I
Than at court, strike spirit into utterance.
At hearing the plaudits of Spain, I am happy;
At finding what I sought, I am gratified;
Since your majesties have exalted me,
I am proud; and pride in service marks
The servant proved. All the quakes and perils
Of the voyage I will not here recount,
But the chilled horrors and phenomena
Of one single day and night I will give,
To serve as the story of every day.
It was night, our starboard was badly struck;
The ship was filling, the heavens confused
Our eyes, while the north star jumped from side
    to side

COLUMBUS.

Of the needle. All the spars and rigging
Were on fire, but all unburnt. The pumps sweated
With great effect throughout the night, but dawn
Displayed the death scowl of mutiny
Upon the dogged decks. Knives flashed, holy names
Were thundered and the ocean seemed to climb
Upon itself, and with it dragged us. Then
Headlong downward, a bound, and all was changed.
The ocean was changed to land to the limit
Of the eye. But joy was changed to panic.
The land was but a seaweed scum upon the sea.
Imagined rocks hurled madness through the ships.
Thirst and water famine, a broken rudder
And creaking timbers renewed the death yell
Of mutiny. That was a night and day.
But we have survived, and land was found.
    Discovery's one thing, possession's another.
In one tragic moment, provoked distrust
Might dispossess us. The gods and the laws
Of this new land must stand beside our own
Until the false foundations of usage
Have thawed before the glow of Christianity.
The new account opened in the national
Ledger, will in time record stupendous
Dealing. Honesty being a draft at sight,
With the confiding natives, embarkation
Must be debarred to all but honest men.
The haberdasher must not extort bullion
For his buttons, nor the cake vender jewels
For his melting sweets. Your royal heed will
Correct corrupt adventure. Your majesties'
Empire abroad shall count additional
Degrees in our next report. May you both live
To see its utmost limits, and may those limits
Outlive us all.

FERDINAND.

Columbus, this day the hired orator
Is out of work. Piping speech is silenced
By the thunderous acclamations of all Spain.
Law is set aside for the people's action,
And action is the bone of history.

FERDINAND.
>Your pleasure is the complement of our joy,
>But time now is trenchant, and will sever
>Us a while. Meanwhile get ready for the sea
>Again. Adieu, Columbus!

ISABELLA.
>Columbus, my best wishes and adieu!

BEATRIX (*Rushing forward from the door*).
>Columbus! You are betrayed! Conspiracy!
>Beware!
>>(*She is hustled off*).

COLUMBUS.
>Lay not hands upon her! A rhapsody
>Hath cleft her lips! Joy hath dazed her!
>Lead her to the open air! Your majesties,
>Only a joyous interruption from
>A surcharged rapture. Long live the King
>And Queen of Spain and their empire abroad!
>(*Music—Grand March, as the curtain drops*).

SCENE.—*A Street (by-way) in Barcelona. Enter* OVANDO,
BOBADILLA, ROLDAN, AGUADO *and* DE OJEDA.

OVANDO.
>I do hate the pretentions of this fellow,
>Columbus. Seeing that his hungry bones
>Were eating through his rags, a plunge for life
>Was needed. He chanced to find some islands
>And has crazed the world with false reports.
>The sharp, grease-soaked mendicant foreigner,
>Now swaggers to court with the proud titles
>Of Admiral and His Excellency.
>What has the blood of Spain come to, when beggars
>Rank front of nobles before the King?

BOBADILLA.
>'Tis true, but some sober heads are left.
>We can discredit the brazen impostor
>And his barren rocks, from which he pirated
>These amphibious beings called Indians.
>The question is, are we all united
>For his overthrow.

ROLDAN.
>Yes; we swear it.

DE OJEDA.
>Then I say, bravely stake your united services
>With the King for any expedition abroad,
>Which he may project.

ROLDAN.
>What, as sailors?

OVANDO.
>Certainly not.

AGUADO.
>Nor as cooks?

BOBADILLA.
>No sir; as discoverers.

OVANDO.
>That's the word. It fits firmly to our fancy.

DE OJEDA.
>Yes, and my oath the devil may sue for
>If I don't find a better tailored people
>Than those mermaid savages kidnapped.
>By Columbus.

BOBADILLA.
>That pirate has discovered nothing, except
>That Spaniards are a flock of geese.

OVANDO.
>Geese with teeth to bite, when suspicion prompts.

BOBADILLA.
>To give him a fall, we must give him a lift.
>Before the King we must lift the fellow
>Upon the shoulders of our influence,
>And make a show of friendship. Kings' pets
>Like old maids' cats need petting, when you would
>Fill their places.

AGUADO.
>Roldan is not in the log-book secret.

BOBADILLA.
>Then out with it, and let him in.

AGUADO.
>Roldan, your ears must not covet a whisper
>From your lips. Dead secrecy. Through Ignacio's

AGUADO.

    Juggled artifice, we have secured
    A copy of the log and bearing of the road
    To the so-called Indies. With it, our fortunes
    Are sure to float.

OVANDO.

    Here comes Ignacio himself.

ALL.

    Bravo! Welcome, Ignacio.

BOBADILLA.

    What's the news?

IGNACIO.

    Most distressing news, but most refreshing.
    The plunging and shouting of Beatrix
    In the presence of royalty, have thrown
    Columbus into a mortal rage.
    The incident singes off his chaste repute.
    When his relations with Beatrix
    Reach the ear of the Bishop Fonseca
    Who is to administer Indian affairs?
    The inexorable prelate will rate
    The Indies as rubbish, alongside
    The sighs of dishonored confidence.

OVANDO.

    Fonseca is our wedge. There is not in Spain
    A sterner will than his.

DE OJEDA.

             That quarter's all right.

BOBADILLA.

    One quarter more will halve the battle.

IGNACIO.

    From all quarters the wind of jealousy
    Shall play upon him. That he does not hate
    This woman, is not in doubt; but doubly
    Proved we have it he will not marry her.
    He is the sun in her soul's meridian.
    But woman's worship, and broken idols
    Fall together. Fallen idols are despised.
    Ere this idol crumbles to unwelcome trash,
    I'll mask it in the mind of Beatrix
    In hideous eclipse and dazzle her soul

IGNACIO.
>With one glimpse of undissembled love ;
>So well dissembled, it will be love in looks.

BOBADILLA.
>Excellent. Your purpose is to the very point.
>It will toss and tangle up Columbus
>And make patch work of his plans.

OVANDO.
>With equal skill, let each plot out his part.

ROLDAN.
>Ready we are as ravenous tigers
>Starved on mice. Nor shall we doze off deeds
>Like sleepy saints, who dream of heaven in bed,
>And reach the church when all the prayers are said.
>(*Enter old* PROFESSOR *passing hurriedly along*).

IGNACIO.
>Hallo, admiral!

PROFESSOR.
>I'm in haste. Can't stay.

OVANDO.
>Your Excellency! don't go. What's your haste?

PROFESSOR.
>A discovery. Going to the Queen with a discovery.

BOBADILLA.
>Hold, bold navigator, what is the discovery?

PROFESSOR.
>A frog. He is in this box.

ROLDAN.
>A frog! That beats Christopher's Indians.

PROFESSOR.
>He has a tendency to talk,
>A tendency to whiskers,
>A tendency to walk,
>In a pair of skinny slippers.
>He has a tendency to chills,
>A tendency to dimples,
>A tendency for pills,
>Which redden all his pimples.

ROLDAN.
>Bravo, admiral! Bring the frog along.

ROLDAN.
We shall swim him in a bowl of amontillado.

PROFESSOR.
Am bound on business; can't go.

ALL.
Come along, Christopher; we can't part with you.
(*He is hustled off*). [*Exeunt*].

SCENE.—*Cadiz.* COLUMBUS *and his brother* DIEGO.

COLUMBUS.
We must trust the methods and memory
Of no man. See for yourself that the fleet
With essential trifles is well supplied.
The general equipment lacks but better looks.
The boatswain's, joiner's, and the caulker's kits
Inspect. Tools, even to a canvas needle,
And broken glass for scraping spars, should be
In instant reach. Have flint and steel beside
Saltpetre spunk, but apart from oil and grease.
See that the doctor's physic is not all ink
And half-dead Latin. Cast an eye, but pry not
Into the providence or poverty
Of the reverend fathers, and note well
The stock of rosaries and holy books
On board. Above all give extravagance
To music, for wind and string implements
Are weapons in a warring sea. Spare strings
Provide for snaps, and a snap for danger then.
To catch to-morrow's flood, to-morrow's work
Must be done to-night. This sunset must find
Every man on board.

DIEGO.
                    Redoubled bustle
In the fleet, will afford the sun spare time.

COLUMBUS.
See that bustle does not play with discipline.

DIEGO.
The method of your orders well establish that.

(*Enter a sailor much excited*).

SAILOR.

 In breathless haste I come to give the news
 That four sweating hands laboring on the pumps
 Of the worthy Nina scarcely serve
 To keep the craft afloat.

COLUMBUS.

     Good news. Better now
 Than to hear it upon the helpless seas.
 Diego, reach the scene at once, and rush
 A score or more of men upon the work.
 If the leaks are not too low give the boat a pitch.

DIEGO.

 She shall be, before to-night, as sound as port
 Bearing the crust of time.   (*Exit*).
      (*Enter* BEATRIX *unexpectedly*).

BEATRIX.

 Columbus! O, Columbus! intrusion
 Pity. I bring no distracting sorrows,
 To flash you into anger or remorse.
 Heaven directed footsteps have borne me here
 From Barcelona, to bathe my failing heart
 In consolation. Not with cares and grief
 Come I, to plead for by-gone loves, long dead.
 Nor come I with claims in forced dictation.
 It was joy alone that allured he here
 To hear the salvos of national glory
 Thundered at your departure. You are free
 As the mountain torrent to bound and shimmer
 In the sunshine of fame. The happiest woman
 Am I, to be a witness in the crowd.

COLUMBUS.

 O, Beatrix, could mine eyes pierce upward
 To the throne of heaven, should I not ask
 With unflinching gaze, have I not courted
 The dismal side of life—its trials, dangers
 And disappointments—all to make amends
 For repented deeds. The cross I have planted
 In new-known lands, whence some stray pilgrim's
   prayers
 May reach the ear of heaven, and descend
 In chastening blessings upon us both.
 A dead wife hovering in my thoughts.

COLUMBUS.

Reciting my oath not to marry again,
Strikes down my will, just when strong to act.
A dead wife wronged, to deceive a living one,
Would be but setting the scales with two wrongs
To balance each other.   When conscience groans
    loud,
The grinding sorrows of remorse, and years
Of rigid sacrifice must be endured.

BEATRIX.

Endured I have, a relentless judgment,
And have sorrowed myself alone.   My hopes,
As a taper that hath burnt itself out
Have flickered away to be enkindled
No more.

COLUMBUS.

                    Beatrix, to all that are born
A punishment is assigned—all transgress
Most grievously.   A multitude of dread woes
Discharge themselves in an angry kindness
Upon us, to promote our better safety.

BEATRIX.

Should woes still sterner than any I have known
Darken round me now, a sweetest joy
They'd be, if their welcome would but lighten
Your heart for the daring voyage before you.

COLUMBUS.

My heart indeed is now enfeebled; crushing
Is the love you unburthen on that heart.

BEATRIX.

Take it with you, for with such buoyant freight
The very waves for joy will sparkle.

COLUMBUS.

I would have the sparkle on your looks,
Rather than on the waves.

BEATRIX.

On my beads of prayer the light of heaven
Sparkles, and wakes vitality in withered hopes.

COLUMBUS.

Prayer and faith are the lock and key of heaven.

BEATRIX.
But outside of cloisters they quickly tarnish.
COLUMBUS.
Then give them a cloistered sanctuary,
And in sweet conserving piety they will not spoil.
BEATRIX.
I thought of that, and then I thought anew,
But the thought that conquered, thought alone
of you.
COLUMBUS.
Thoughts are sometimes not our own. Mine belong
To Spain alone. Lives she has given me
To pilot safely to the new-known world.
Not enough are all my thoughts for that.
BEATRIX.
Then let our thoughts flit free, but let our love
At anchor ride.
COLUMBUS.
Love should be changed to friendship, and friend-
ship
Should act as if it were in love.
BEATRIX.
That is the love that is most enduring.
Time and your thoughts are not your own.
I will, therefore, depart with an urgent word
Of caution: Traitors.
(*Enter officer and guards with* ESPINOSA *under arrest*).
OFFICER.
This daring criminal in the very act
Of tampering with the charts was caught.
BEATRIX.
Villain he is! a slimy fiend! scourge him!
I will swear him to death!
COLUMBUS (*Takes* BEATRIX *aside*).
This is public business. Beatrix withdraw
With grace.
BEATRIX.
Traitorous rogue.
COLUMBUS.
Do, for my sake, withdraw and meet me,

COLUMBUS.

For an important conference to-morrow.
                    (*Kisses her hand and bows her off*).
Hands off the prisoner! I know the man,
And will fathom his intent myself.
Your duties demand your time; waste it where
It is wanted.   [*Exeunt officer and guards*].
Espinosa, what is your answer to the charge?

ESPINOSA.

I secretly heard that one Don Ignacio,
A mortal enemy of yours, had bribed
A knavish sailor to steal important
Charts and memoranda from the ship.
Without your orders, I made them doubly safe,
And without reserve this is my offence.

COLUMBUS.

A misunderstanding. That is enough.

ESPINOSA.

Danger to your person I shall now divulge.
That same railing woman whom you hurried
From this spot, is plotting with Don Ignacio

COLUMBUS.

Believe you so, by all that's sacred?

ESPINOSA.

I can prove it. Come with me and you shall see
    them
Both in fervent, damnable consultation.
The plot is deep. She and Ignacio will stretch
It from Spain to San Salvador.

COLUMBUS.

Hath lightning struck 'gainst lightning, or hath
Thunder silenced the voice of thunder, or have
Sight and hearing both deceived me?
Let us see.   [*Exeunt*].

SCENE.—*A chamber.* BISHOP FONSECA *and* BOBADILLA.

FONSECA.

He who finds a gold mine and jealously
Reserves his right alone to root its worth,
Robs the world of glittering expectation
And disputes with providence the plaudits

FONSECA.

    Of discovery. And with Columbus
    Thus it is.

BOBADILLA.

    With jealousy in one eye,
    In the other greed, his inward interest
    Seizes what it sees.

FONSECA.

             That I will not affirm.
    When the oceans were in rags, Columbus
    Was in them. His hearth-stone at home sighed
      for him,
    Whilst the wet-flapping rags lashed him.

BOBADILLA.

    Columbus is no coward, nor wet-spunk.
    He's a storm-bird hatched from the impetuous
  - Elements of our nature. He will whirl
    Whither the winds will blow him. No coward;
    His life is a hazard.

FONSECA.

             Nor is he self-serving.
    Selfishness is another name for safety.
    It thrives upon the dread of risk. 'Twas risk,
    And death pale risk, that carried him beyond
    The reach of help.

BOBADILLA.

            I sorrow for his faults.
    The faults of most men fall upon themselves
    His, make an abortion of his own work
    And bring pangs of disappointment to all.
    His royal sponsors with the very church
    Itself are shocked.

FONSECA.

    To ascertain his motives, his actions,.
    We must follow, then our action shall follow his.

BOBADILLA.

    The Spanish colonies in your sacred hands
    Will grow to empires.

FONSECA.

    Indian affairs shall grow if growth is in them.
    Insubordination and arrogance
    Shall not be suffered to stunt them.

BOBADILLA.

The indispensable man knows no master
Until his equal to a master yields.
No better sailor than Columbus lives,
But as pupils often excel their teachers,
We may have men in Spain—I know we have—
Who can streak the ocean with a hundred lines
At angles to the Santa Maria's course.
These lines may reach to regions far outside
The calculations of brave Columbus,
And make his discoveries but a playground
To vast empires yet unknown.

FONSECA.

Bobadilla,
It breeds us second youth to find men like you.
Tax your instincts with possibilities
So sublime. Every man in Spain I vow
Who has ambition's fangs wisely fastened
To his enterprise shall have equal chance.
Whom it may offend I care not.

BOBADILLA.

How, should jealously blow its windy voice
Upon the scales, to turn it against justice?

FONSECA.

When the common house-fly laps a ferment
In the nascent stage he saves the whole world
Perhaps an epidemic. Likewise a keen watch
Upon the lips of jealousy may arrest
The influence of a pestilential breath.

BOBADILLA.

Your words sparkle with the cherished notions
Of the King. They will have a triumphant
Seconding from all the enterprise of Spain.

FONSECA.

I think, Bobadilla, Indian affairs
Lit up by your luminous fancy, would soon
Make the King's notions sparkle in a new light.
I'll see the King about you ; your counsel
Would assist us much at Cadiz.

BOBADILLA.

In return for your friendship, I offer
To find a hundred men fitted to lead
Expeditions to the Indies.

FONSECA.

But Columbus most steadfastly objects
To yield us copies of his charts and journals.
He claims that he alone must guide the traffic.
Such a beggarly commerce would not feed
The hungry cats of Catalonia.

BOBADILLA.

Leave the charts and journals to me. Money
Will find them in the market. Mankind's strange
Incorrigible curiosity hath
Already made parlor pictures of them.

                                   (*Enter Courier*).

COURIER.

Most sage and reverend administrator,
I ask in the King's name privacy to speak.

FONSECA.

Bobadilla, rejoin me in an hour;
I have something of further consequence
To say.   (*Exit* BOBADILLA).

COURIER.

                    Urgent instructions from the King
I bring. The brother of Columbus
Is hourly expected at Valladolid
From the Court of England, where he has been
Negotiating in the Discoverer's
Behalf. Your presence at Valladolid
Is needed to sift suspicions of base
Bargaining between King Henry Tudor
And Columbus. By word of mouth I give
The King's commands to save delay and seal
Dispatch with secrecy.

FONSECA.

We are surprised if there is no surprise.
I have no answer to instruct you with
Beyond saying that all necessary steps
Shall be taken at once. With posting speed
Unbroken, we shall reach the court in time.

COURIER.

In a lighter saddle I now shall sit
Being unweighted of this grave affair. To spur
The return road I leave your gracious presence
And say Adieu !   [*Exit*].

FONSECA.
-              Best blessings and adieu!
Honest Diogenes! since the search began,
Has your lantern flashed 'pon an honorable man?
                              (*Exit*).

SCENE—*Court at Valladolid.*   (QUEEN ISABELLA *and*
                    BEATRIX.

ISABELLA.
On his return I shall acquaint Columbus
Of your visit to court, to see the young
Precocious pages, and your own little son
In particular.
BEATRIX.
              Your royal words weigh more
Than all the earth with Columbus. Your heart
And touching words in my cause will win him
Out of all excuse.
ISABELLA.
Yes; if pleased he looks,
I will do more than speak. I will display
In manner, the charm of your society;
But in matters resting with his discretion
I dare not approach him. His strong will
Would resent dictation even from me.

BEATRIX.
Inspiring pleasure from your words he will sip,
And sap them to his heart. Enough
Is well contained in your majesty's
Good intentions.
ISABELLA.
In transacting with Columbus officially,
It is not deemed in taste, to pry into
The proportions of his domestic nature.
His reverential warmth of speech, with his
Illumined presence, seems true evidence
Of goodness of nature.
BEATRIX.
He so loved his wife; she is never dead.
At times he thinks of her, and then of me;
Then of his promise not to marry again;

BEATRIX.

And thus he vibrates between two forces.
The poor negative force, I, would be willing,
But for young Fernando, to weaken down
My claim.

ISABELLA.

You want a friend, and friendship seldom fails
When woman to a woman's heart appeals.
You love Columbus; the ocean loves him too;
But oceans are weak contending with you.
In your cause I shall act the double part
Of advocate on both sides, and umpire
Between the two. Flood your thoughts with sunshine
And clouds will glow with rosy tints.

(*Enter* PRINCE JUAN, BARTHOLOMEW, COLUMBUS, *and the two young pages*).

JUAN.

Your majesty in the temporary
Absence of the King, the honor reverts
Happily to me of presenting to you
Bartholomew, a distinguished brother
Of our illustrious friend, Columbus.

ISABELLA.

As a guest of the realm, we welcome you.
The hospitality and freedom of Spain
Are yours; not because of the name you bear,
But for personal worth, which heralded
Accounts credit you with. If Bartholomew
Cannot become a Christopher, he will prove,
I hope, no less a Columbus in devotion
To our throne.

BARTHOLOMEW.

Your kind majesty, the salt ocean leaves
But little sweetness upon a sailor's lips;
I cannot, therefore, phrase acknowledgments
In ringing measure. But in plainest speech
I say I am your servant where hardship,
Sacrifice, danger, or death demands me.
At this royal audience, attention
I would direct to a possibility,
Lurking at the Court of London. Whilst there,

BORTHOLOMEW.

    I found two Brothers Cabot, playing round
King Henry's flag, to catch a waft of sanction,
For some adventurous scheme. It may be,
That these great and daring navigators
Would like to measure off some claims on your
Rich golden Indies. On incidents noted,
This suggestion is based, and is submitted
From sense of duty.

ISABELLA.

    Your vigilance brings us timely warning.
All necessary agencies shall be
At once invoked for our protection.
This service shall go on record.

BARTHOLOMEW.

    Your most gracious majesty, I thank you
For all royal favors, not the least of which
Is the honor conferred by assigning
My two young nephews to the royal suite
Of the Crown Prince Juan. But, who is this!
Beatrix Enriquez a maid of honor?

ISABELLA.

    Of honor made she is; though not our maid
Of honor. Honored we are by her presence.

BEATRIX.

    Her majesty will excuse our greetings
Bartholomew. Renewal of our friendship
Must take place outside the court.

BARTHOLOMEW.

    I hope your presence here has the approval
Of my brother. From his lips I soon shall know.

ISABELLA.

    Bartholomew, the Admiral's wishes
For your return being happily realized,
We commission you to proceed at once
To Hispaniola to relieve him
And free his time for explorations in
The neighboring lands. A small flotilla
Is at your command, subject to orders
From our India office.

BARTHOLOMEW.
If navigation can outstrip the wind,
The wind shall trip behind us in our speed
And the Admiral with early freedom
From his cares, can stake his lengthy mileage
With the holy cross, into the rich heart
Of the golden regions. But ere I go,
One favor I must ask : it is, that you
Retain in your kind and royal custody
These two children, until with voice or pen
The Admiral demands your gracious
Surrender of them.

BEATRIX.
These children fondle to two voices only,
A third would grate the strings of harmony
And make existence a plague of discord.

BARTHOLOMEW.
Impute not mischief, when absent interests
Are in point.

BEATRIX.
Affected vindication of these interests
The court ignores. I represent those interests.
You are but an agent, self-installed.

ISABELLA.
Children and kindred alike are subjects
Of the crown. Therefore, this contention must
Be ruled by us.

BARTHOLOMEW.
I submit.

BEATRIX.
And so do I.

ISABELLA.
Then rich with expectations let us part,
Let life be a heaven to our heart,
Let false words never make a false step lame,
And rob not a leaf from the chaplet of fame.
Long live Columbus! The Queen's best wishes
Carry to him Bartholomew. Adieu!

BARTHOLOMEW.
Long live the Queen! and may I live to hear
Her magic voice once more.

                                    [*Exeunt*].

ACT III.

The Alhambra Palace (interior). Ferdinand *and* Isabella *(enthroned).* Present—*Nobles, Prelates and
Court Dignitaries.* Enter Columbus *and two brothers
in chains.* (Espinosa *is their guard*).

COLUMBUS.
Your majesties, treachery has gone abroad
Instead of staying snugly at your Court.
In this gloomy hour I disown my name
My boyhood that had dreamt of glory,
Could it look down through the lapse of years,
It would blush to see its advanced manhood
In chains and in disgrace. Take back your royal
Honors; spill your frothy promises
In the sink, and give me freedom to sail
Before the mast once more, under an honest
Foreign flag. (Isabella *sobs aloud*.)
FERDINAND.
Silence I say! though you are Columbus.
Your bitter taunts have overpowered the queen.
COLUMBUS.
Overwhelmed I am to find these chains were forged
From her sweet majesty's good intentions,
And from the mysteries of your deep king craft.
Speak not of silence to me. The black night
And hurricane, chains, dungeons and starved death
Could not affright me. Nor can thunders rattled
From your imperial throat make a coward
Of me.
(*He falls fainting. The King lifts him, and helps to
remove his chains.*)
FERDINAND.
Strike the hell-wrought irons from his noble limbs
And case them up for spiteful Bobadilla.
Unrivet the unholy chains
Which degrade his worthy brothers,
And keep them from rust till the miscreants

FERDINAND.

Are dragged from San Domingo home.
Come, Columbus, droop not. Drive the fire of speech
In raking arraignment on the guilty,
But snap not the mettle of the wrong man.
Your enemies are outlaws branded
And irons double weighted shall be their lot.

COLUMBUS.

Your majesties, with zeal and diligence
I have served you, and to gain paradise
I could not have done more. Much more 'tis true
Was possible, but a want of knowledge
And experience found me short at times
When much was needed. I was soldier, sailor,
Judge, and advocate when Bobadilla
Armoured with your proud authority seized me
At San Domingo. I was pinioned
In a musty dungeon, and thence smuggled
On board a caravel, without process,
Accusation, or an exchange of words.

FERDINAND

Bobadilla is a madman.
His soft brain pickled by the ocean air
Has grown prickly. He shall be shipped
For Spain by return sail. This will prove
Our sincerity to you.

ISABELLA.

Columbus never doubted my sincerity.

COLUMBUS.

Never, your kind majesty. But before
This most painful scene is ended, I feel
Forced to say, report informed me that
Bobadilla's credentials, signed by the king,
Gave him power to act.

FERDINAND.

Primed with no credentials went he from here.
Six blank sheets he bore with our sign manual
And no more. You cannot but remember
That you yourself requisitioned us
For a judge and fiscal for Hispaniola,
Complaining sore of duties over-heaped
And all undone, and of lack of time
For survey of terra firma's golden regions.

COLUMBUS.

    I do remember that ill-wished request.
    'Twas turbulence, fraud, and trampled virtue
    That wept it from my pen.

FERDINAND.

    That admission mends the case between us.
    But we must admit a slip of judgment
    In granting free blank sheets to Bobadilla.
    It was our intent that they should be filled
    With stern commands, only when contumacious
    Subjects defied the laws established by you.

COLUMBUS.

    I am satisfied, and all my sorrows
    With the chains have dropped. Since you have
        wisely
    Repudiated Bobadilla's work
    One favor I now demand; it is this :
    That I shall be allowed to lock the irons
    That I have worn, upon the cursed carcass
    Of this treacherous dog Espinosa.

FERDINAND.

    What canon of our sacred law has he degraded?

COLUMBUS.

    He is a fellow whom I had favored
    And befriended, and then in my distress,
    When every man in San Domingo
    Had refused to place the chains upon me,
    He alone jumped perfidiously forward
    To do the ignoble work.

FERDINAND.

    To the dungeons with him; hurl him from our
        sight.

COLUMBUS.

    As a parting favor will your majesties
    Command that my two brothers' chains be kept
    In lustre brightness for the limbs
    Of Bobadilla and rebellious Roldan?

FERDINAND.

    With augmented iron they shall clank
    Penitential music upon these culprits.

COLUMBUS.
Then having our royal friends recovered,
And our dastard enemies discovered,
To the dungeons we shall play the warders
Of this vile Espinosa. We ask no orders.

ISABELLA.
Justice is yours, and your enemies all shall answer.
So far, justice has been done to us at least.
(*All withdraw*).

SCENE.—*A Street. Enter* DON IGNACIO *and* BEATRIX.

IGNACIO.
Lady of profound and guiding judgment
Think you not, that unspeakable misconduct
Has spattered stains upon great Columbus?
Great he was, but now he is greatly less
Than the pettiest thief serving out correction.

BEATRIX.
Sir, give me all the knowledge you possess
Of this shattering news. Some meagre hints
Have given my feverish grief a thirst to know
And realize the worst.

IGNACIO.
He has been adjudged a malefactor
And tyrant, that I know. And detected,
He has been in misrepresentations
Of the wealth of his worthless discoveries,
Which have already wrought stupendous loss
To the nation's treasury.

BEATRIX.
O scorching, maddening woe! The sweet verdure
Of thought is burnt up. Night and day are mixed.
Two worlds, the old and new, have dashed together,
And the proud ruler of one has gone down
In chaos.

IGNACIO.
Sweet sympathetic soul, lose not concern
For yourself, by wasting unavailing grief
On the hopeless reputation of one
Who has skilfully destroyed himself.

BEATRIX.

    Unfold his troubles, but not the troubles
    That trouble slander, for slander can fill
    The whole earth with bubbles from a pipe full
    Of its murky soap.

IGNACIO.

    Most heroic and devoted being,
    Know ye not that Columbus filled the earth
    With gilded bubbles, and that all have burst.
    He loosened the whole world from its holdings
    By announcing the discovery
    Of a land of gold.

BEATRIX.

    Reflect not on his errors which carried no intention.

IGNACIO.

    Errors are criminal when all mankind
    Suffers by them. And his were the errors
    Of an ill-concerted plot.

BEATRIX.

    Errors are but chastisement's messengers,
    We are all acquainted with their visits.

IGNACIO.

    Without dishonour, I confess to errors
    But not to insincerity of speech.
    I am a plain man, proud of honest affluence
    And domestic traits. Joy of life is marred
    By one circumstance alone ; it is this :
    The want of a devoted companion
    Like you to share the ease and luxury
    Of my home.   (BEATRIX *recoils.*)

    (*Enter officer of the law with two guards.*)

OFFICER.

    Prisoners both, surrender to our warrant
    In the name of the king and of the queen.

IGNACIO.

    What is the charge ?

BEATRIX.

    O what is the crime !

OFFICER.
Silence ! No words, and you shall hear the charge.
One Espinosa, who is under arrest
For high treason and conspiracy 'gainst
Their majesties, the king and queen of Spain,
In the person of their exalted viceroy,
Christopher Columbus, hath repented
Of his act and turned king's evidence.
He deposeth that you, Ignacio,
And this woman, Beatrix Enriques,
Are prime instigators of a plot against
Our Sovereigns in the person of their
Viceroy. Therefore we claim you as our
Prisoners.

IGNACIO.
He's a villain ; 'tis false !

BEATRIX.
'Tis false! I am the wrong person. The viceroy
Will liberate me ; tell him who I am.

OFFICER.
No words here ; you can speak in the judgment
hall.
March the Prisoners off.

IGNACIO.
Villain ! Tyranny !

BEATRIX,
Innocence ! Misunderstanding !

[*Exeunt.*]

SCENE.—*Interior of a Church. Tomb of* PRINCE JUAN
in the background. His name cut on it. Enter
REVEREND TUTOR *and Pages (in mourning dress).*

TUTOR.
Children of fortune, the time for parting
Has come for all of us. No prince, no page,
No page no tutor.

DIEGO.
We are pages to the prince ; our tutor
Good father you are.

TUTOR.
>But the prince is dead. * In that royal tomb
>Lie his lifeless limbs.

FERNANDO.
>Is he dead for ever?

TUTOR.
>For ever. His lips that played with language
>Shall welcome us no more. His French *bon jour*
>And Suabian *auf wiedersehen* we shall miss
>For ever.

FERNANDO.
>Could not doctor's physic make him speak again?

TUTOR.
>No; life and death are not on speaking terms,
>Nor can tempering physic reconcile them.

DIEGO.
>Perhaps, in dying he lives an angel.

TUTOR.
>Indeed, he lived to die an angel.

FERNANDO.
>Do angels die?

TUTOR.
>Angels never die. Oft in mortal tenements
>Angelic spirits live, and leave when their
>Sanctified abodes are about to fall.
>Now, in affection, fall upon your knees
>In the dead shadow of this monument,
>And pray that your master, good Prince Juan,
>May receive a crown in heaven, to replace
>That which he left on earth.

They kneel, bent forward at the foot of the Monument.
TUTOR kneels behind them. Ghost of the Prince ap-
pears on the Monument and addresses the TUTOR,
who rises and holds up a cross.

GHOST.
>Man of God, charged with the cure of souls, fear
>Not; 'tis the shade of Juan that speaketh.
>On my death bed a wish I had indulged
>Was stifled off by delirious fever

GHOST.
>Before it was expressed. That wish is this:
>That my two young pages be still retained
>By my royal mother, and appointed
>Pages to herself. Counsel her to protect
>The children of Spain's safest friend,
>The martyred discoverer. And now
>Discharged of a weight oppressive, I charge
>Your faith to enact my wish. Until we meet
>In heaven, farewell. [*Exit.*]

FERNANDO.
>Diego, I thought I saw my father
>Standing upon a distant rock.

DIEGO.
>I saw him, too, and his wrecked caravel
>Drifting away before his eyes.

TUTOR.
>And I saw something, too. But no portents
>Of approaching ill are these illusions,
>Since consecrated ground is known t' inspire
>No unwholesome fears. To her majesty
>We shall now repair and recount experiences.
>   [*Exeunt*].

SCENE.—*A street.* *Enter* SOLOMON *and* MAHOMET (*a Jew and a Moor*).

SOLOMON.
>Bad news is coming in too fast.

MAHOMET.
>Ay, faster than we can stow it away.
>What's the news to-day?

SOLOMON.
>Public alarm has it that the Queen
>Is down with some dangerous malady.

MAHOMET.
>That is a cloud indeed; a storm for some one.

SOLOMON.
>For Columbus assuredly. The Queen
>Is his only friend.

MAHOMET.
All glory and no profit is no fun
For King Ferdinand. Discoveries so far
Have been a loss.

SOLOMON.
And the King will pound his losses out of us.

MAHOMET.
His vengeance will raid our hiding holes and cash.
He will decree wholesale confiscation
Of our decencies of dress.

SOLOMON.
I fear we are catalogued for learned show
In medical museums.

MAHOMET.
Or for the harvest fields to frighten off rapacious
birds.

SOLOMON.
Mahomet, at one time I detested you,
Because you were a Moor.

MAHOMET.
And I hated you because you were a Jew.
Shake hands Solomon ; Christian hatred has
Made us brothers.

SOLOMON.
Well now, taking a long and broad view
Of the situation, what tactics think you
Are the best for our races to hold to?

MAHOMET.
No tactics, I say. An intrenched silence,
With holes to spy through, is our only safety.

SOLOMON.
The new world must be watched. Sterility
In that region would mean stern attentions
For us ; whilst returns in golden treasure
From there, would turn the royal anger from us.

MAHOMET.
Solomon, you are a Solon, and the
Sole one to comfort us.

SOLOMON.
What think you of Bobadilla's blunder?

MAHOMET.

    Bobadilla and Roldan both are drowned;
    Their caravel with all on board went down
    In a storm.

SOLOMON.

    I know. They were the wiliest enemies
    Columbus had.

MAHOMET.

    This Espinosa under sentence of death
    Is just as sly a traitor.

SOLOMON.

    Among the mysterious characters
    Before the public, there seems none more noted
    Than Beatrix Enriquez. She was falsely
    Arrested and released. But fright hath whizzed
    Her mind to wandering. For information
    Of her whereabouts, royalty offers
    A slipper full of coin.

MAHOMET.

    Columbus hath pledged himself to this woman,
    And new worlds cannot release him.
    He who discovers a woman's love, I say,
    Will never surpass his discovery.
    And he who unsettles a woman's heart,
    Throws tripping stones in his own path of life.

(*Enter officer and guards with a dozen Moorish and
Jewish prisoners manacled*).

OFFICER (*to* SOLOMON *and* MAHOMET).

    Two more prisoners. How strayed you from your
    Precinct to these outer bounds?

MAHOMET.

    To soothe a sickly friend.

OFFICER.

    That answer will not do. These prisoners have
    forged
    The same story. Handcuff these Moors.

SOLOMON.

    I am no Moor; I am a Christian.
    He is the Moor!

MAHOMET.
> He is no Christian—no Christian at all—
> He is a Jew!

SOLOMON.
> Yes; I am a good Christian searching for
> Beatrix.

OFFICER.
> A Jew and a Moor; march the prisoners off.
> > [*Exeunt.*]

SCENE.—*An open space in Zaragua. Hispaniola, in front
of a building. Numerous Caciques with their fol-
lowers armed, stand in the background. OVANDO with
Soldiers and Spanish hidalgos in front. Acrobats,
Showmen, &c.*

OVANDO (*to Caciques*).
> Generous chiefs, throw down your arms and with
> > cheer
> Respond to the holiday created
> For you. Advance not for war nor council,
> But to witness the pranks and merry games
> Of our native land. With hearts, bound forward!
> Bring loosened speech and trusting footsteps into
> Play with sportive Spaniards—all children
> For the day. Past provocations you shall drown
> In richest wine within this banquet hall.
> Your enemy Columbus is not here to-day.
> > (*Caciques advance, throwing down their arms*).

OVANDO.
> Let the games begin!

(*A square is formed; acrobats and showmen make displays*).

OVANDO (*aside to Confidant*).
> Stratagem and slaughter! These savage chiefs
> Kill out our best designs. Now is our time
> To kill their power with death. Note this signal:
> When I touch this charmed emblem on my breast,
> Seize and rush them quickly to this so-called
> Banquet hall. Then with flaming brands burn them
> Hall and all.

(OVANDO *ascends a throne to witness the games. Exit confidant to instruct the soldiers. Caciques are seized and burned within the building,* OVANDO *folds his arms and enjoys the conflagration.*

OVANDO.

In one hour we have secured peace for ever.
Timid Columbus would have bequeathed to Spain
Eternal war.

SCENE.—*Country road.* BEATRIX *carried in a sedan chair by two armed Carriers.*

BEATRIX.

Hold, I say! and tell me if I am free,
Or if this is some device for infamy
Or death?

1ST CARRIER.

You are more free than we. Protected freedom
Has been bestowed on you.

BEATRIX.

By whose authority am I protected?

2ND CARRIER.

By the dead Queen's express instructions.

BEATRIX.

Hath harassing calamity carried
Reason with it?

1ST CARRIER.

You know good lady that without reason
Cruel arrest was inflicted on you,
And that, since then you have, in feverish dread
No doubt, wandered beyond the ken of friends.
Even the town crier hath given you up.

BEATRIX.

Into importance I have sprung in
Hope's expiring moment.

2ND CARRIER.

The pet of many and the friend of all
You are. And more than all, great Columbus,
Who is now housed in sickness, raves aloud
His love for you.

BEATRIX.

Columbus! that name was once a joy.
I do not forget the name.

2ND CARRIER.

He does not forget you. A hundred times,
It is rumored, he bellowed to his attendants
To summon you to his side. Your absence
From the city was concealed from him,
Fearing distress would aggravate his malady.

BEATRIX.

He asked for me? Yes, it often happens
That love ignites in one as it expires
In another. It will expire again in him.

1ST CARRIER.

It will burn at least until you arrive;
Then let us pursue our journey.

BEATRIX.

What road is this? Whither does it lead?

2ND CARRIER.

It is the straight road to Valladolid.

BEATRIX.

Is that where Columbus is?

2ND CARRIER.

Yes; there he is waiting and sighing for you.

BEATRIX.

Then proceed. I think I would like to see
Him once again.

1ST CARRIER.

If the Admiral could hear you say that,
He would launch again for another discovery.

2ND CARRIER.

All ready; off! Double step!

[Exeunt]-

SCENE—*A darkened Bed Chamber. Crucifix, Candles, and Font on Small Table beside a large Arm Chair on which* COLUMBUS *sits in a dying condition.* COLUMBUS *and his son* DIEGO. *They repeat alternately the Deprofundis.*

COLUMBUS.
Any tidings yet of your brother's mother,
Beatrix Enriquez?

DIEGO.
She is nowhere to be found. Search is vain
In Valladolid.

COLUMBUS.
An hour ago a reverend father
Told me that he had heard of her return
To the city.

DIEGO.
Then I shall impress some diligent friends
Into a hasty search.

COLUMBUS.
To see her, is the last joy of life
I yearn for. Let her sweet face be the last
Object my dying eyes shall behold;
United with her I then shall die.

DIEGO.
With no impossibilities to stay,
You shall see her without delay.   [*Exit.*]

COLUMBUS.
Soon I shall discover another world,
My dying eyes weakening away from this,
Grow steadfast on the world to come. In vain
I look for the parting pleasure of life,
The presence of the woman who loved me,
And on whom I have inflicted years of anguish.
The incessant clamor of life, shattered
And silenced the sweet whisperings of love.
Home and workman's comforts I might have had
But irresistible destiny forced me
To another course. That course was wrong,

COLUMBUS.

    For ingratitude, toil, and enmity
    Fill my measure of reward—deserved reward,
    For having aggrandized a king
    Who has forsaken me. But the holy cross
    I have carried to the helpless heathen
    And the true King will not forget my reward.
    Life grows weaker and conscience sterner.
    O Beatrix, come! ere dying reparation
    Leaves my voice. But surge not the parting
        moments
    Into anger. Life ebbs. It will be too late.

(Sinks back into his chair and sits silently some moments.)

(Enter DIEGO DE DEZA, *Archbishop of Seville.)*

COLUMBUS.

    Many welcomes to your grace.

DEZA.

    May many times that welcome be pronounced.
    How thrives it with you now, Columbus?

COLUMBUS.

    Still sinking and resigned. Ere you entered
    A horrible vision flashed my closing eyes.
    Methought I saw a wailing multitude
    Of Indian Chiefs encompassed by fagots
    And raging flames. Ovando seemed to fan
    The hot holocaust, with satisfaction
    In his face.

DEZA.

    Ovando I fear will prove a Bobadilla
    In indiscretion. Your vision is perhaps
    Of true enactment.

COLUMBUS.

    Your grace, these moments teem with agonies.
    Mismanagement of the Indies; the King's neglect,
    The death of the sweet good Queen Isabella,
    And worse than all, the absence of Beatrix.
    One moment's holy union, and the sight
    Of this long forgotten ring, glistening
    On her finger, would light up my soul,
    And chasten it for Heaven. *(Enter* DIEGO.)*

DIEGO.
Joy, dear father, we have found her.

(*Columbus with emotion rises from his seat. Enter Beatrix·
Overcome by the touching scene, she becomes incapable
of speech. Gazing at Columbus she approaches him.*)

Columbus and Beatrix take each other's hand, and
regard each other, apparently transfixed. Columbus,
with the ring in his hand, places it on the finger of
Beatrix, and then sinks back dead. Beatrix kneels,
with her forehead resting on his knee, while the Archbishop holds his stole over them, and invokes a bless-
ing.

www.ingramcontent.com/pod-product-compliance
Lightning Source LLC
Chambersburg PA
CBHW021223260626
47172CB00002B/572